For Fraser

This paperback edition first published in 2013 by Andersen Press Ltd.
First published in Great Britain in 1995 by Andersen Press Ltd.,
20 Vauxhall Bridge Road, London SW1V 2SA.
Published in Australia by Random House Australia Pty., Level 3, 100 Pacific Highway, North Sydney, NSW 2060.
Copyright © Ruth Brown, 1995.
The rights of Ruth Brown to be identified as the author and illustrator of this work have been
asserted by her in accordance with the Copyright, Designs and Patents Act, 1988.
All rights reserved. Colour separated in Switzerland by Photolitho AG, Zürich.
Printed and bound in Singapore by Tien Wah Press.

10   9   8   7   6   5   4   3   2

British Library Cataloguing in Publication Data available.

ISBN 978 1 84939 632 5

This book belongs to:

...........................

04262921

# GREYFRIARS BOBBY

## Ruth Brown

ANDERSEN PRESS

"I'm fed up with
sightseeing," moaned Tom.
"It's too hot and I'm thirsty."
"Well, you're in luck," said Becky.
"Here's a fountain. Have a drink."
"It's a drinking fountain for people and dogs," said Tom,
reading the inscription.
*A tribute to the affectionate fidelity of Greyfriars Bobby.*
*In 1858 this faithful dog followed the remains of his*
*master to Greyfriars Churchyard and lingered near the*
*spot until his death in 1872.*

"Let's go into the churchyard," said Tom.

"Do you think we would have seen Bobby the dog if we'd come in here a hundred years ago?"

"Of course you would," said the gardener. "He'd have been lying in the sun in this special place that was his home for the last years of his life.

Back then, you would have found him sound asleep, dreaming of the
days before he lived in the churchyard.
Those were the days when . . .

. . . Bobby used to help his master, Old Jock, guard the cattle, which were brought into the city each evening for the market the following day.

The story goes that, in the mornings, after work, Jock and Bobby would visit the cafe owned by Mrs Ramsay, who would always save special titbits for Bobby – a bone, a bun or even a piece of pie.

On their rare days off they'd walk for miles in the hills where
Old Jock had lived as a boy.

But in the winter they would stay in the city, still guarding the cattle despite the freezing winds and bitter cold that eventually made Old Jock so ill that he died.

And, on a grey morning, Bobby followed his master for the last time – to the churchyard of Greyfriars.

He got as close as he could to Old Jock and that's where he stayed.
But how cold and hungry he was that night, huddled against the great,
granite stones. He remembered the café – if he went there by himself
would there still be a bone, a bun or a piece of pie saved for him?

Of course there was – and when
Mrs Ramsay found out where
Bobby was living, there was food for him
every day. The people were so touched by the loyalty of the
little dog that they looked out for him and looked after him.

He was given his own engraved collar, and water bowl,
and, best of all, official permission to live in the churchyard –
and that's where he stayed for fourteen years,

until, finally, he too was buried there – near his beloved master, Old Jock."

"What a story," said Becky.
"Aye," agreed the gardener. "Bobby never forgot his old friend."
"I don't think we'll ever forget Bobby," said Tom.

# Also by Ruth Brown:

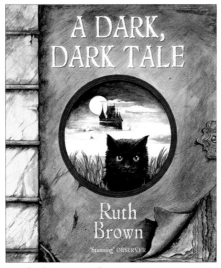

9781842709894

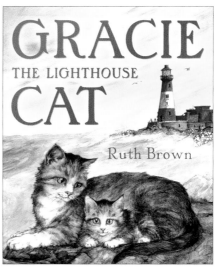

9781849390262

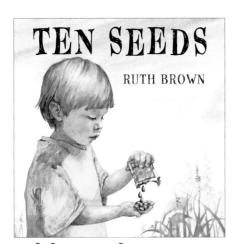

9781849392518

9781849392280

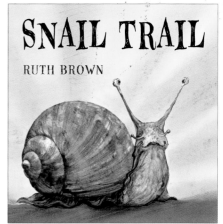

9781849392525